For Elisabeth
—J.G.

To my mother
—P.M.

THIS IS A BORZOI BOOK PUBLISHED BY ALFRED A. KNOPF

Text copyright © 2016 by Jeff Gottesfeld
Jacket art and interior illustrations copyright © 2016 by Peter McCarty

All rights reserved. Published in the United States by Alfred A. Knopf, an imprint of
Random House Children's Books, a division of Penguin Random House LLC, New York.

Knopf, Borzoi Books, and the colophon are registered trademarks of Penguin Random House LLC.

Visit us on the Web! randomhousekids.com

Educators and librarians, for a variety of teaching tools, visit us at RHTeachersLibrarians.com

Library of Congress Cataloging-in-Publication Data
Gottesfeld, Jeff.
The tree in the courtyard / by Jeff Gottesfeld ; illustrated by Peter McCarty. — First edition.
pages cm.
Summary: "The story of the tree outside of Anne Frank's window." —Provided by publisher
ISBN 978-0-385-75397-5 (trade) — ISBN 978-0-385-75398-2 (lib. bdg.) — ISBN 978-0-385-75399-9 (ebook)
[1. Trees—Fiction. 2. Frank, Anne, 1929–1945—Fiction. 3. Jews—Netherlands—Fiction. 4. Holocaust, Jewish (1939–1945)—
Netherlands—Amsterdam—Fiction.] I. McCarty, Peter, illustrator. II. Title.
PZ7.G6939Tr 2015
[E]—dc23
2014044007

The text of this book is set in 18-point Perpetua.
The illustrations were created using brown ink on watercolor paper.
Illustration on page 36 based on photo of Anne Frank seated at desk [Anne Frank Fonds Basel/Premium Archive/Getty Images].
Reproduced by permission of Getty Images and the Anne Frank House.

MANUFACTURED IN CHINA
March 2016
10 9 8 7 6 5 4 3 2 1

First Edition

The Tree in the Courtyard

Looking Through Anne Frank's Window

BY **Jeff Gottesfeld**

ILLUSTRATED BY **Peter McCarty**

ALFRED A. KNOPF · NEW YORK

"The two of us looked out at the blue sky,
the bare chestnut tree glistening with dew,
the seagulls and other birds glinting with silver
as they swooped through the air, and we were
so moved and entranced that we couldn't speak."

—Anne Frank

The tree in the courtyard lived for
172 years.

She was a horse chestnut. Her leaves
were green stars; her flowers foaming
cones of white and pink. Each fall, she
let spiky seedpods clatter to earth. In
winter, her bare boughs etched a lattice
against the pale blue sky.

She grew near a city canal. Seagulls
flocked to her shade.

For the first part of her life, her world
was the courtyard. She was not yet
tall enough to see beyond the homes,
workshops, and factories. Then one
spring, she stretched above the orange
roofs and took in the beautiful city.

She spread roots and reached skyward
in peace.

Until war came.

Explosions shook the ground; rockets split
the night. Strangers invaded the city.

The first winter of the war, a new owner came to
one of the factories.
He had a wife and two daughters.

The older girl was quiet and proper. The younger was lively, with dark hair. When they visited the factory, she would play by the canal or write by the kitchen window. She wrote for hours. Even when her father called her, she wrote.

The tree loved the sight of her.

In the heat of midsummer, the girl stopped coming. The tree dropped
worried leaves until she spotted the girl in the factory annex. Her family was
there, too. A father, mother, and a boy soon joined them. Later, another man.
And a black cat.

The girl and her father stitched ragged curtains for the main windows. From time to time, a face might peer out between the cracks.

The only clear view was into the attic. There, the girl would read, stroke the cat, and brush her unruly hair. Sometimes she stared at the sky. Mostly, she wrote.

She filled a red-and-white diary.

When warplanes roared and bombs rocked the annex, the girl fled into her father's arms.

She did not come outside. The tree did not understand. The war dragged on.

Once, through the curtains, the tree watched the people light candles and sing.

The girl grew pale and thin. A young woman helper who worked in the factory brought her pens and paper. The girl wrote and wrote some more. She filled page after page.

The fourth winter of the war, the tree saw the boy with the
girl. They would talk and laugh, or simply gaze out the attic
window at her bare branches glistening with dew, so moved
and entranced that they couldn't speak.

They kissed.

The tree made her blossoms extra
bright that spring.

Late one summer morning, men in gray uniforms came to the factory. They ripped the curtains from the annex windows, dumped the girl's papers to the floor, and herded the people into waiting black cars.

The cars sped off.

The woman from the factory gathered the girl's writing.
The tree kept a vigil.

Summer, autumn, winter, spring. The seasons changed.

The war ended. Only the father returned. He was
thin, with sad eyes, as he padded through the annex like
a living ghost.

The woman helper gave him the girl's writing. They cried.

The tree lived on. But she was never the same.

Time passed. To her surprise, other children came to the annex. They walked where the girl had walked, and sat where she had sat. Some found a windblown seedpod on the pavement, or gazed at the tree, so moved and entranced that they couldn't speak.

Year after year, they came.

By the end of the century, the tree had lived a full life. She was ready to die.

Many strangers came to try to save her. They injected her with medicine. They trimmed her crown and cut sprouts from her trunk. They built her a steel support and collected her seedpods like gold coins.

The tree recalled how few had tried to save the girl.

The summer the girl would have turned eighty-one,
a storm snapped the tree's trunk in two.

Just like the girl, she passed into history.
Just like the girl, she lives on.

Her seeds and saplings have been planted with love. One grows in New York City, where twin towers once stood. Another grows at an Arkansas high school. Still more grow in England, Argentina, France. . . .

All around the world.

Though the new trees are still young, children come to visit. They read the girl's words—about a chestnut in a courtyard glistening with dew—and touch the thin trunks.

They are so entranced that they cannot speak.

AFTERWORD

The girl is Anne Frank. During the occupation of the Netherlands, the Nazis deported all the Jews they could find to concentration camps. Anne and her family hid in the rear annex of her father's factory at 263 Prinsengracht in Amsterdam. Until their betrayal and arrest on August 4, 1944, they were kept alive by several of the factory workers, including the woman helper, Miep Gies. After they were taken away, Gies collected and saved the notebooks and pages of Anne's diary.

Anne died of typhus at the Bergen-Belsen concentration camp in March 1945, three weeks before that camp was liberated. Otto Frank, Anne's father, was the only survivor from the annex. After the war, Gies returned the diary to him; he arranged for its Dutch publication. The diary first appeared in print in June 1947 and was published in America in 1952. Since then, it has been translated into seventy languages and remains in print.

The diary refers to Anne's sewing of window curtains (July 11, 1942), her frightened reaction to air raids (March 10, 1943), and a communal Chanukah celebration (December 7, 1942). She mentions the horse chestnut tree three times. The quote at the start of the text is from her entry on February 23, 1944.

Despite a ten-year effort to save the aging tree, she collapsed and died in the summer of 2010. Saplings from the tree have been planted at the following American locations, notable in the quest for freedom and tolerance:

- National September 11 Memorial & Museum, New York, New York
- Central High School, Little Rock, Arkansas (1957 desegregation struggle)
- Capitol Hill, Washington, D.C.
- The Children's Museum of Indianapolis, Indiana (Anne Frank Peace Park)
- Sonoma State University, Rohnert Park, California (Holocaust & Genocide Memorial Grove)
- Southern Cayuga School District, Aurora, New York (Harriet Tubman home; Women's Rights National Historical Park)
- Holocaust Center for Humanity, Seattle
- Boston Common, Boston, Massachusetts
- Holocaust Memorial Center, Farmington Hills, Michigan
- Idaho Anne Frank Human Rights Memorial, Boise
- Clinton Presidential Center, Little Rock, Arkansas

Other saplings and seedpods from Anne Frank's tree have been planted around the world.